A WILD TV Show

My sincere thanks to the *Channel Ten Totally Wild* team for their time, information, images and enthusiasm for this book.

Dear Reader

One day before school I watched the ***Totally Wild*** TV show with my nine-year-old grandson, Jackson. We couldn't stop watching all the amazing adventures and animals. The show's reporters were having so much fun, too.

THE PIGS SHOOK THEIR HUGE BODIES JUST LIKE DOGS DO AND THEIR SMELLY MUD COVERED ME!

PIP RUSSELL – *TOTALLY WILD* REPORTER

On that day, I decided to write a book about the ***Totally Wild*** show. It has been a lot of fun.

I was lucky enough to meet with the ***Totally Wild*** reporters, crew and production staff. I hope you enjoy reading about these talented people as much as I enjoyed writing about them!

Sharon Parsons

NELSON
CENGAGE Learning™
For learning solutions, visit **cengage.com.au**

Contents

A WILD TV Show

Adam and Pip with a snake

the camera films turkeys

canoe polo

Adam in the video tape library

1 A Wild TV Mission

A *Totally Wild* Sneak Peek

WILDERS

People who watch the *Totally Wild* TV show.

Hello Wilders!

Join me on a mission to find out how the *Totally Wild* TV show is made. It's been top-secret until now – but we're able to take a peek behind the scenes to find out what really happens.

Amazing Places

Colin interviewing in a cave

Action Adventures

Adam billycarting in a race

Underwater Adventures
Pip swimming with sharks
Sean sandboarding
Slippery Animals
Always Fun
Extreme Sports
Nat with a snake
Tess skydiving

A *Totally Wild* TV Reporter

Pip Volunteers in Africa

Pip Russell is one of the *Totally Wild* TV reporters. I talked to Pip before she went on a six-week adventure in Western Kenya, Africa – without TV crews. On that trip, Pip worked as a volunteer for World Youth International.

Pip Russell in an F111 jet

AN INTERVIEW WITH PIP

Q: Why are you going to work in Africa?

A: I like what World Youth International is doing in Africa to help children and families.

Social Studies

World Youth International

In 1988, Robert Hoey, a 21-year-old Australian, began a non-profit organisation for young Australians called World Youth International. Australians who are 18 years or over can apply to work as volunteers. They help people in countries such as Kenya, Uganda, Nepal and Peru. Their work improves the education and lives of children and families.

Pip in Africa

Pip eats WORMS!

Q: How did you feel about being on TV for the first time?

A: I wasn't too scared. I pretended that the camera was one kid – I didn't think about all the kids watching! I was just being myself.

Q: Did you like learning motocross?

A: I loved it. I picked it up quickly – changing gears and speeds, cornering, even standing up – all so easy.

Q: How did you feel about bungy jumping?

A: I felt really nervous and I felt sick! It took me 20 minutes to get up enough courage to jump. And when I jumped, I screamed my lungs out!

Q: What was your muddiest story?

A: For the rare pigs story, I had to wash the smelliest mud off pigs! After I sprayed them with water, they shook their huge bodies just like dogs do. Their smelly mud covered me! I laughed a lot that day.

Pip learns to motocross

Before the Camera Rolls

From Ideas to TV Scripts!

Story Ideas Created
The team meets to suggest ideas to the series producer.

Story Ideas Approved
The series producer chooses which stories will be on the show.

Story Ideas Prepared
The production coordinator writes the new story ideas on the whiteboard.

Story Scripts Written
The segment producers or the TV reporters write the scripts. Each script can take hours to research and write.

At Home With Adam

PRESENTER: ADAM COX	
INTERVIEWEE: Mark and Diane Bruhn	**PRODUCER: ADAM COX**
DATE: 25 June 09	**SENT TO INTERVIEWEE:** yes / no
RELEASE FORMS:	**FILE VISION:**
PAINTBOX: ordered 00.00.00	**VISION RELEASE:**

SYNOPSIS: Adam takes the TW cameras back to his folks farm.
PROMO SOUND UP: Duration: no longer than about 10 sec
INT/PTC/VO - A snippet that encapsulates the story or elaborates on synopsis.

PTC 1 G'day Wilders, today I have something very special and somewhat personal. I'm going to give you a behind the scenes tour...of my place!	*Adam drives into driveway* *Delivers piece from car* *Drives towards property*
Music up 4 – 5 secs	*Cuts of Farm animals* *Adam driving in*
INT 1 **Alright, well let's start where it all began. Hi Mum!** *Adam greets mother* **Say hello to the wilders!** Hello etc **This is where I get my height from...** **What's that?** Well I thought the viewers would like to see photos This one and this one... **Okaaaay thanks for that mum...** You need to clean you're room.. **Yeah I've been meaning to do that**-*Adam leads mum away before he runs for it*	*100%* *Exiting car* *Mum is revealed* *Cutaways of two pics* *100%* *Cameraman running with camera pov(ground shot)*

first page from a TV story scrip

How to **Write** a TV **Story Script**

Research for the Script

- **Research:** Research the topic on the Internet and in reference books, and then write notes.
- **Complete the Script Checklist:** Check the location for filming and the date.
- **Write Interview Questions:** Before interviewing the talent, write questions that start with: "Who", "What", "Where", "When", "Why" and "How".
- **Interview the Talent:** Ask the talent questions and write notes.

TALENT

Talent are the people who appear in each *Totally Wild* story.

Prepare for the Script

- **Title:** Write a short title.
- **Synopsis:** Write one to three sentences about the story.
- **Story Angle:** Write ideas to interest and entertain viewers.

Write the Script

- **Introduction:** Write something that will "hook" the viewers in to watch the story. What you say or show must happen in the first three to five seconds.
- **Middle:** Write about short, interesting and fun events to keep viewers watching the TV story.
- **Ending:** Write a funny and exciting ending.
- **Music and Sound:** Write notes where music and sounds can be added later in the edit suite.

Edit the Script

Proofread the Script: Make sure the sentences are short. This helps the reporter to tell the facts quickly and clearly. This also helps the viewers to understand the content.

Read the Script

Read the Script Aloud: The words will be spoken on TV so read the script out loud. The script should sound natural, interesting and fun.

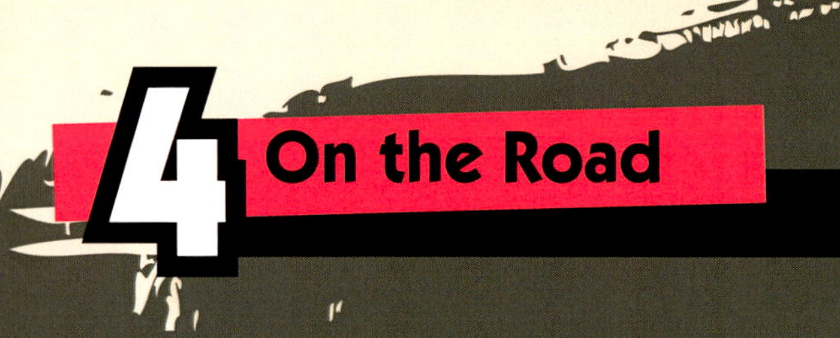

4 On the Road

The Crew and Author on Location

While Pip was on her adventure in Africa, I met *Totally Wild* reporter Adam Cox.

That day, we drove to Adam's family farm with his camera operator, Lucas, and sound recordist, Ashley. There we would film our first story, called "At Home with Adam".

As we drove to the farm, we talked about some of their *Totally Wild* adventures.

Adam in the Totally Wild *4WD*

The Worst Animal to Film

When I asked what was the worst animal to film, they all said loudly, "Horses!"

"Why?" I asked.

Ashley said, "They don't like anything above their head, so when I put the long microphone above the horses, they become spooked."

THE MICROPHONE UPSETS THE HORSES BECAUSE THEY CAN BUCK. THAT'S DANGEROUS FOR THE CREW.

ADAM COX

Camera Operator Hates Spiders

Lucas hates spiders! He told a scary spider story.

"One day, we were filming in the dark Rockhampton Caves for eight hours with lots of huge, hairy huntsman spiders. That was a long, scary day!"

Cheeky Monkeys

Ashley told a funny story about an orangutan in Borneo.
It crept up behind Ashley, stole his bag, and ran up a tree!

His next story was about a cheeky monkey who stole the "fluffy". It was hard to get back because the monkey played with it.

FLUFFY

A sock that fits over the microphone to reduce wind noise.

Almost There

When we were five minutes from Adam's farm, the crew explained why they had the best jobs.

"We get paid to have adventures in the coolest places around Australia!" says Adam.

"And … I get to record all kinds of sounds, from extreme machines to the biggest sounds on Earth!" adds Ashley.

"And at the weekend, when people go away on adventures, I enjoy staying home for a rest!" laughs Lucas.
Finally our vehicle stopped at the entrance to Adam's family farm.

Ashley and Lucas unpacking equipment

5 On Location – Adam's Farm

Working as a Team

At Adam's family farm, the team talked about the script – **what** would be filmed, **when** it would be filmed and **how** it would be filmed.

BEFORE Each Scene

Lucas (camera) and Ashley (sound) move to the best place for the shot. When Lucas starts filming, he says to Adam, "Whenever you're ready, mate."

DURING Each Scene

Lucas and Ashley are silent. Only Adam speaks to the camera. Then Lucas might say, "Stop. Thanks mate, beautiful."

Each scene is filmed twice so Adam and the editors can choose the best takes, or scenes, back at the studio's edit suite.

Adam with his mum and the crew

AFTER Each Scene

Adam asks questions like these:

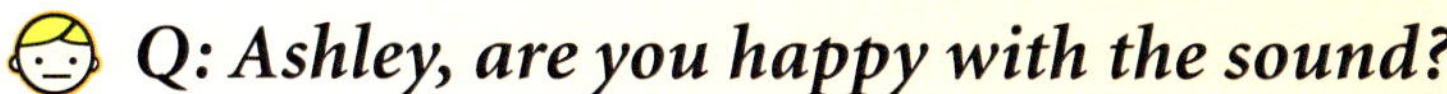

Q: Ashley, are you happy with the sound?

A: Yes, a plane flew over at the end but we can edit it out.

Q: Do you want another shot of that, Lucas?

A: No thanks, mate, I just need a cutaway.

Ashley may ask Adam a question like:

Q: Do you need any sound-ups?

A: Yes, the turkeys gobbling would be good.

CUTAWAY

A shot of something other than the main subject. If the reporter is talking about turkeys to the camera, a cutaway may be a shot of just the turkeys.

SOUND-UPS

The recorded sounds to be used in the story. For example, if Adam is talking about turkeys, their gobbling sounds will be recorded separately.

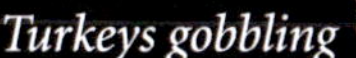

Turkeys gobbling

PACK UP AFTER All Scenes

After four hours of filming, the crew packed up and drove for an hour to the next story about canoe polo. Join the crew in Chapter 6 to find out how to play canoe polo.

A Wilder's **Response** for a ***Totally Wild*** TV Episode

TEXT TYPE
Response

My name is Jackson and I'm in Grade 3. My class watched an episode of the children's show *Totally Wild*. The episode was about one of the reporters, Adam, who went to his family's farm for the day. As class reporter, I was asked to write a response about the episode and ask people in my school what they thought of it.

In the episode, Adam visited his mum on her farm. They also filmed many animals on the farm and Adam told us lots of interesting information.

filming Adam arriving at his farm

setting up the equipment to film the story

Ashley checks the sound.

Lucas says, "Action!"

filming Adam talking to the turkeys

I asked four kids in my school to write what they thought of the episode so we could send it to the people at *Totally Wild*.

"Hi *Totally Wild*. I watch your show every morning before school. My mum used to watch your show when she was a kid. It is the best show. See you tomorrow on TV." Olivia – aged 6

"I think that Adam's awesome!" Jack – aged 9

"I love your show, it rocks! From your highest fan." Jamie – aged 10

"My twin brother and I watch your show before we go to school. Keep up the great show!" Nicholas – aged 11

filming Adam running away from his mother

I thought the episode was really interesting. I watch *Totally Wild* all the time and I'm a fan of Adam. It was great to be able to see where his family are from and where he grew up. I loved the turkeys – they were so noisy that they made me laugh!

On Location – Crashing Canoes

All About Canoe Polo

It was a cool, dark night in Brisbane. As I walked with Adam and the crew towards a floodlit pool, we heard the loud sounds of canoes crashing and canoe polo players calling out to their teams. Every player desperately wanted the ball.

I saw canoe polo players pushing the other team's canoes to try and tip them over.

five players per team

players paddle fast

SAFETY TIP

When a player has trouble doing the Eskimo roll, they should bang on the canoe to alert others for help.

Health and Sport

The Eskimo Roll

Canoes can roll over many times during a match, so canoe polo players need to learn the Eskimo roll. This involves being able to "roll" the canoe back upright again quickly.

It's not easy – as Adam the reporter found out!

What Is Canoe Polo?

Canoe polo is a "paddle, catch and throw" game – a cross between basketball, soccer and water polo.

- Teams: There are two teams of five players. There are no set positions for four players; the fifth player is the goalkeeper.
- Time: It's a 20-minute game – a ten-minute first half, a five-minute break and a ten-minute second half.
- Paddle: A paddle is used to push a canoe away, to flip the ball over to a team player, or to dribble the ball.
- Dribble: Players dribble the ball by throwing it forward and then paddling up to it.
- Goals: Goals can be shot from anywhere in the pool.

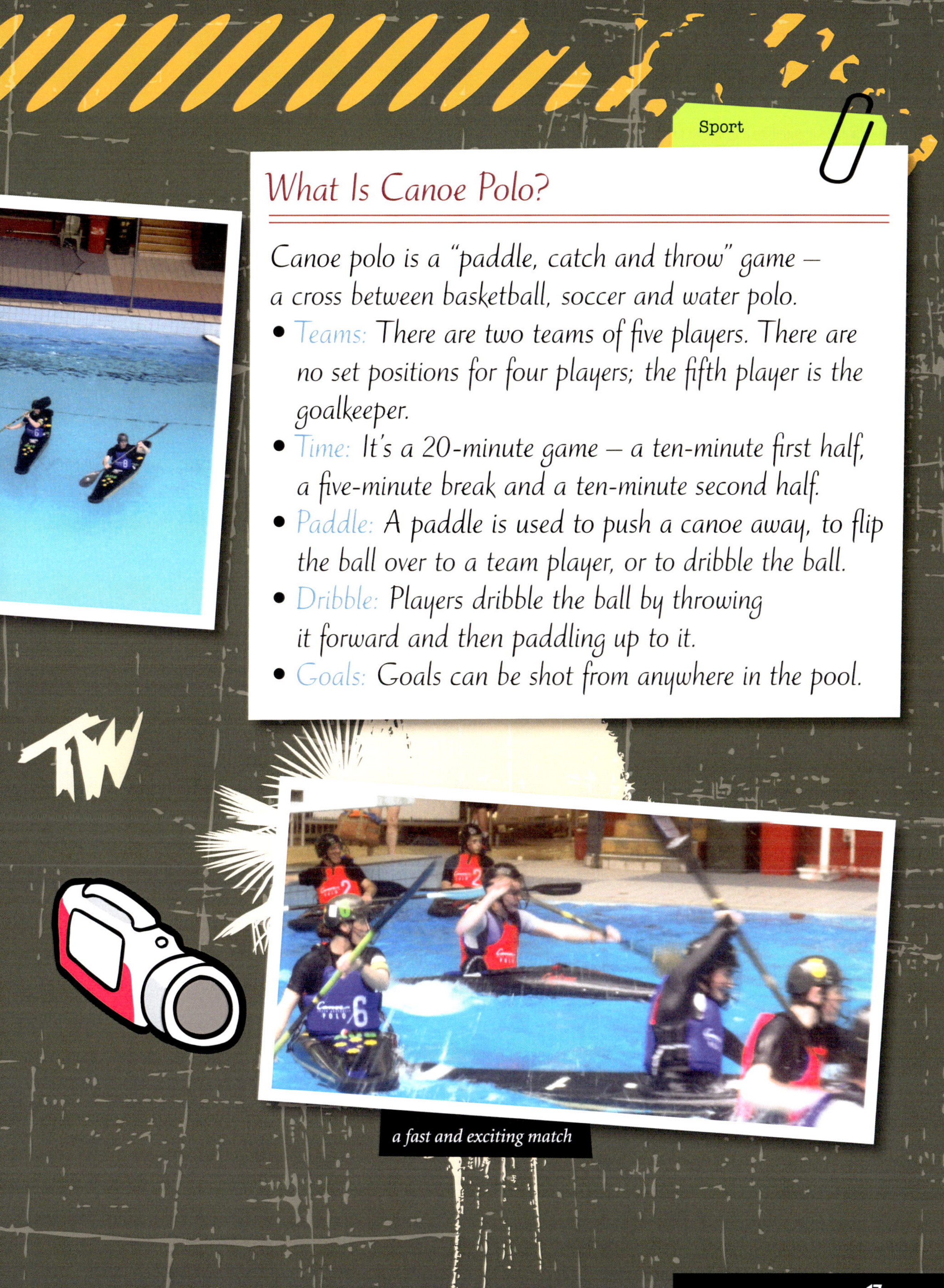

a fast and exciting match

Adam's **Canoe Polo** Story

Adam begins his story

At the Beginning

Adam begins the story resting in his float ring in the pool and says to the camera, "Ahhh, nothing beats some time out in the pool. It's a chance to unwind, relax and reflect on ..."

But suddenly the whistle blows and a ball lands next to Adam.

In seconds, canoe polo players crash into Adam. Surprised, he says, "Hey! What the ... ?"

The coach calls out, "Adam! What are you doing?"

"I thought this was a leisure pool!" he replies, with a puzzled look.

"No mate, tonight this is the sports pool, and you've landed yourself in the middle of a game of canoe polo!" laughs the coach.

"Canoe what?" Adam asks.

"Canoe polo! Jump out and I'll get you sorted!"

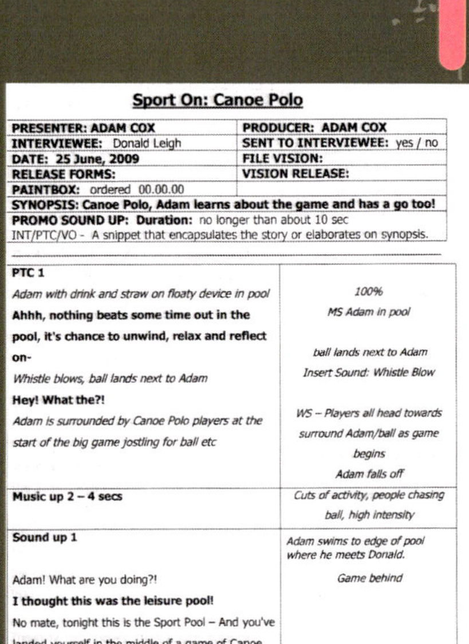

Sport On: Canoe Polo

PRESENTER: ADAM COX	PRODUCER: ADAM COX
INTERVIEWEE: Donald Leigh	SENT TO INTERVIEWEE: yes / no
DATE: 25 June, 2009	FILE VISION:
RELEASE FORMS:	VISION RELEASE:
PAINTBOX: ordered 00.00.00	
SYNOPSIS: Canoe Polo, Adam learns about the game and has a go too!	
PROMO SOUND UP: Duration: no longer than about 10 sec INT/PTC/VO - A snippet that encapsulates the story or elaborates on synopsis.	

PTC 1 *Adam with drink and straw on floaty device in pool* **Ahhh, nothing beats some time out in the pool, it's chance to unwind, relax and reflect on-** *Whistle blows, ball lands next to Adam* **Hey! What the?!** *Adam is surrounded by Canoe Polo players at the start of the big game jostling for ball etc*	*100%* *MS Adam in pool* *ball lands next to Adam* *Insert Sound: Whistle Blow* *WS – Players all head towards surround Adam/ball as game begins* *Adam falls off*
Music up 2 – 4 secs	*Cuts of activity, people chasing ball, high intensity*
Sound up 1 Adam! What are you doing?! **I thought this was the leisure pool!** No mate, tonight this is the Sport Pool – And you've landed yourself in the middle of a game of Canoe Polo! **Canoe what?!** Canoe Polo! Jump out I'll get you sorted!	*Adam swims to edge of pool where he meets Donald.* *Game behind* *Helps Adam out of pool*

a page from Adam's canoe polo script

IN A THREE-MINUTE STORY, THE KIDS WATCH US LEARN COOL NEW THINGS, CHALLENGE OURSELVES AND ... HAVE HEAPS OF FUN!

ADAM COX

FILM TALK

PTC: piece to camera

VO: voice-over

At the End

After playing the canoe polo match, Adam paddles towards the camera and says, "Well it's only been 20 minutes but I am exhausted! Still there's no doubt this sport is an absolute ball!"

The Twist

Suddenly a ball hits Adam on the head and his canoe tips over. **"Oh!"**

Epilogue

Adam was new to canoe polo but in one hour he had learnt enough to play the sport for his TV story.

7 Back at the Studio

A Photographic Journey

The next day, Adam works in the studio on his two stories – "At Home with Adam" and "Canoe Polo". He works "offline" to choose the best "takes" or scenes. These "takes" then become the post-production script for the editor's work.

Technology and Arts

Film Talk

Offline: this involves choosing the best "takes" for a post-production script.

Post-Production: this relates to editors' tasks when putting the story together, such as music and sound effects.

Adam's Post-Production Tasks

Adam works offline at his desk.

Adam works with the sound engineer in the edit suite.

Adam does voice-over work.

Adam is in the tape library to pick out vision for the editor.

8 A TV Story – Start to Finish

A 16-Hour Story

Every three-minute *Totally Wild* story takes about 16 hours to produce. Many people work as a team to produce exciting stories for children to watch. So what are the main things that happen over those 16 hours?

Adam in a bungy bullet

1 2 3 4

> FIRST FOUR HOURS

Jobs Before Filming

Story Idea Decided
(the whole team)

Story Script Written
(producers and reporters)

TV Crew Organised
(production coordinator)

5 6 7 8

> NEXT FOUR HOURS

Filming the Story

Crew On Location
(reporter, camera operator, sound recordist, producer)

Pip in an F111 jet

Sean in a zorb ball

Tess kneeboarding

Colin after the mud challenge story

9 10 11 12 13 14 15 16

> LAST EIGHT HOURS

Jobs After Filming

Post-Production

Story's footage is checked offline (reporter, editor)

Sound in Edit Suite

Voice-overs recorded, and music and sound added (reporter and sound engineer)

Master Tape

Finished, checked, edited and approved (producers)

Story is added to an episode (series producer)

Adam reporting on parasailing

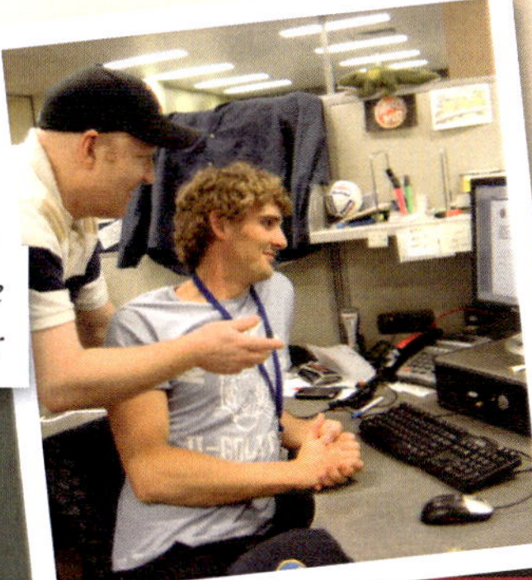

Adam and the series producer

Natalie reporting on aerial antics

Ready for Screening on TV

Master tape is ready for screening on TV for children to enjoy!

> "EACH EPISODE LASTS FOR 24 MINUTES. IT'S LIKE A PUZZLE, TRYING TO FIT A VARIETY OF EXCITING THREE-MINUTE STORIES INTO 24 MINUTES!"
> SERIES PRODUCER

Index

Glossary

edit suite	An area where technology is used to assemble the different parts of a TV program, such as sound and images
floodlit	Brightly lit, by placing powerful lights around the area or person being filmed
master tape	The original tape carrying the images and sound for a TV program (which is then copied)
non-profit	An activity that is carried out without the purpose of making money
piece to camera	A part of a TV program where a presenter talks directly to the camera as if it were his or her audience
sound engineer	The person responsible for ensuring that sounds and voices are recorded clearly
vision	The pictures of people, action or scenes that are used in a TV program
voice-over	A part of a TV program where someone explains or introduces something, but is not seen on the screen